MARILYN'S MONSTER

MARILYN'S MONSTER

MICHELLE KNUDSEN   ILLUSTRATED BY MATT PHELAN

CANDLEWICK PRESS

Some of the kids in Marilyn's class had monsters.
It was the latest thing. Marilyn didn't have a monster.
Not yet. You couldn't just go out and get one.
Your monster had to find you.
That's just the way it worked.

Some kids woke up to find their
monsters had chosen them
while they slept.

Some kids got their monsters
on the way home from school.
Or on the bus.
Or in the park.

Timmy's monster chose him right
in the middle of a history test.

At first Marilyn wasn't even worried about it. Eventually her monster would find her, too. There were still a bunch of kids who didn't have monsters yet.

But then Franklin got his at the library.

And Rebecca got hers while riding her bike.

And Lenny got his while he was running away from some mean older kids who kept picking on him.

Nobody picked on Lenny
anymore after that.

After a while, Marilyn was the only one left without a monster. She knew she wasn't supposed to try to look for him. But she kind of did anyway. She hung around the library, hoping.

She poked around the playground, pretending not to look under the slide and behind the climbing bars. She watched the others with their monsters, playing and laughing and having fun and never being alone.

At night, when her room was dark and scary, Marilyn thought about how good it would be to have her monster there beside her.

"We're sure you'll get your monster soon," said her parents.

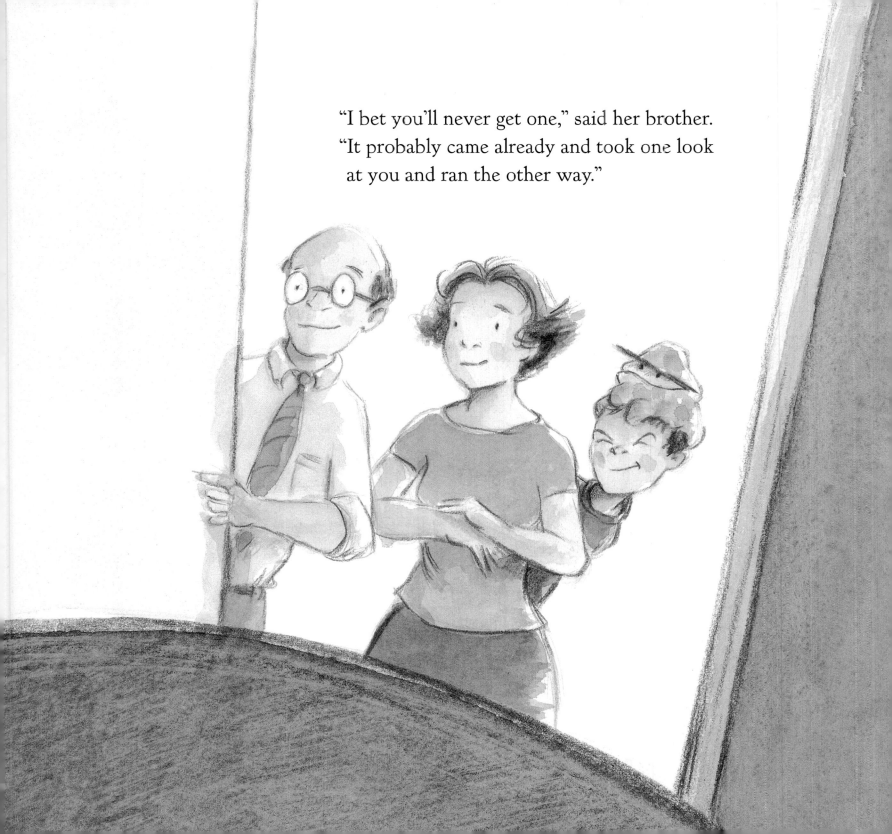

"I bet you'll never get one," said her brother. "It probably came already and took one look at you and ran the other way."

Marilyn tried to be patient. She tried to believe her monster was still coming. She made sure she brushed her hair very carefully every morning and wore pretty clothes and smiled a lot and tried to look very friendly and interesting and smart and fun to be around. She tried to be the kind of girl no monster could resist.

But at the end of the week, her monster still hadn't come.
She was afraid that maybe her brother was right.

Marilyn went out and started looking.
She didn't just *kind of* look. She *really* looked.
She looked as hard as she could.
She searched behind the stone lions
that sat outside the library.

She checked beneath the
benches at the playground
and the park.

"Maybe I'm better off without a monster," she told her friend Deborah at school. "They seem like a lot of work."

"Hmm," said Deborah. She didn't really seem to agree.

"Maybe your monster's just running late," said Margaret.

"Maybe it's invisible, and it's been here all along, and you didn't even notice," said Jerome.

That night in her room, Marilyn whispered into the scary dark.

"Are you invisible? Have you really been here all along?"

But if her monster was there, he didn't say so.

Marilyn stopped trying to seem pretty and nice and friendly and fun all the time. She stopped looking around in the library and the playground after school. She started feeling mad. Where was her monster? What was taking him so long?

She was so mad, sometimes she thought maybe she really *didn't* want a monster. What was so great about monsters anyway?

But they were pretty great. She could see that they were.
She wanted one more than she could say.

"That's it," Marilyn said one morning. "I'm going to find my monster."

"You can't," said her brother. "That's not the way it works."

"Maybe," said Marilyn. "But you don't really know. Maybe my monster is different."

She put on her good walking shoes and packed a thermos of juice and a peanut butter and banana sandwich. Then she made a second sandwich and put that in her bag, too.

She went down the winding path through the woods
and out into the big field with the wildflowers.
She didn't see her monster.

Marilyn stopped in the middle of the field. She closed her eyes and stood very still. She thought about trying to sing a beautiful song like those princesses in movies did sometimes that made all the little animals come and sit on their shoulders. She thought about trying again to be patient and wait and hope that her monster would find her someday soon. Then she took a deep, deep breath and shouted in her loudest, loudest voice.

And then, very softly, she heard a voice say, "Here."

Marilyn followed the voice. It was very quiet, but she could hear it very clearly. She followed it across the field and into the woods on the other side and over to a tall, tall tree.

And there was her monster, half hidden among the leaves.

"I got lost," her monster said in his small, soft voice.
"And then I got scared. And then I got stuck."

Her monster had two long, lovely wings. They were
tangled and caught in the branches.

Marilyn climbed up and, very gently, helped her monster get free.

"I kept hoping you would come and find me," her monster said.

"I'm sorry it took me so long," Marilyn said back.

Then they sat there together and had peanut butter and banana sandwiches and juice.

When they were ready, Marilyn's monster lifted her up
and flew her all the way back home.

"Oh, honey!" said her parents. "Your monster found you at last!"

"We found each other," Marilyn said.
She and her monster smiled together.

"It's not supposed to work that way," her brother said.

Marilyn just looked at him. She didn't think he was right about that. She thought there were a lot of different ways that things could work.

And that night when Marilyn went to bed, the dark didn't seem so scary. Marilyn wasn't sad, or afraid, or lonely. She was happy.

Marilyn's monster was, too.

For some of my favorite friends:
Emily, Alex, Maddie, Sophie, Evie, and Tommy

M. K.

To all the amazing friends I've found or who have found me

M. P.

Text copyright © 2015 by Michelle Knudsen
Illustrations copyright © 2015 by Matt Phelan

First paperback edition 2017

Library of Congress Catalog Card Number 2014944904
ISBN 978-0-7636-6011-6 (hardcover)
ISBN 978-0-7636-9301-5 (paperback)

17 18 19 20 21 22 APS 10 9 8 7 6 5 4 3 2 1

Printed in Humen, Dongguan, China

This book was typeset in Kennerly.
The illustrations were done in watercolor and pencil.

Candlewick Press
99 Dover Street
Somerville, Massachusetts 02144

visit us at www.candlewick.com